NOT ANOTHER CHRISTMAS!

by Joan Fitzgerald

Illustrated by Elizabeth Uhlig

Marble House Editions

Published by Marble House Editions
96-09 66th Avenue, Suite 1D, Rego Park, NY 11374

Library of Congress Cataloguing-in-publication data

Fitzgerald, Joan
Not Another Christmas!/by Joan Fitzgerald

Summary: Disillusioned with today's seemingly materialistic children, Santa decides instead to take a vacation, a decision he later regrets.

ISBN 0-9677047-4-x
Library of Congress Catalog Card Number 2004104849

Printed in China

This book is dedicated to

Jake and Lindsay

Santa was tired and cranky. He slouched in his favorite chair near the fireplace, surrounded by pillows.

"My rheumatism hurts and I've had a cold since Thanksgiving. I can't face another Christmas! I've been Santa for hundreds of years and I'm simply too old now to fly over the globe distributing gifts. I've done my share," he complained to his wife.

"But if you don't do it, who will be Santa?" she asked as she lifted a pumpkin pie out of the oven.

"Hmmph!" he replied. "I do love pumpkin pie! Let someone else carry on. It's about time! Anyway, the reindeer are in no shape to fly. Prancer has a sore leg, Dancer is lame and Blitzen has fleas."

"The children will be disappointed. They expect you to bring them presents."

"Kids have too many things today as it is. Electronic games, calculators and computers, bikes and skateboards. There isn't a child alive who doesn't have a bedroom stuffed with the latest gadgets. They don't need me!"

"Please think it over," Mrs. Claus begged as she set a mug of hot cider in front of her husband.

1

"My mind is made up! I'm going on vacation. All year I spend day and night, out in the workshop with the elves, putting toys together. I need a rest!"

"But where will you spend your vacation?"

"We're going to Florida!" he cried. "Sun! Sand! Blue water! Get busy and pack!"

While his wife reluctantly packed their clothes, Santa got his old Model T car out of the barn.

"But what will we do?" asked the elves as they watched the two climb into the car.

"Feed the reindeer! Put liniment on Prancer! Play checkers! I don't care. We'll be back in April. I'll send you a postcard from the South."

Flakes whipped around their car as the Clauses drove over the snow-packed country lane. They arrived at a small town where they boarded a bus to Fairbanks, Alaska. The bus was slow and the weather was wickedly cold, but Santa didn't care.

"I'm going away! I can hardly wait to get a tan!" he chortled.

Mrs. Claus said nothing. She didn't want to go to Florida.

In Fairbanks, they were able to get seats on a jet plane bound for Chicago. Santa was wearing an old brown suit with a blue tie under his worn, plaid overcoat so no one recognized him.

When they landed at O'Hare Airport in Chicago, they had a two-hour stopover. Mrs. Claus sat primly in the waiting room while Santa wandered all over the airport, his blue eyes twinkling.

Then they boarded another jet for Miami beach.

"Maybe I'll do some deep sea fishing," Santa mused, as they strapped on their seat belts.

They landed in Florida many hours later and took a taxi to a hotel near the beach.

"Feel that warm air! Look at the sunlight!" Santa cried. "I'm going to get right into my swim suit and go to the beach!"

In their room, Santa donned his red and green striped bathing suit, which came down to his knees and covered his elbows. Snapping a red bathing cap over his shaggy, white hair, he left for the beach.

Mrs. Claus was worried. "I don't think he knows how to swim," she fretted. "What if a shark bites him? Oh, I wish we were back at the Pole!"

But Santa was having a wonderful time. He rented a rubber raft and pushed it into the water. Then he spent the afternoon bobbing up and down, watching the sailboats out on the ocean.

"Why haven't we done this before?" he wondered.

When Santa returned to the hotel, he dumped a pile of shells on the bed. "Tomorrow we're going to Oceanland to watch the dolphins put on a show!" he informed his wife.

They left the hotel early in the morning and took a bus to Oceanland, where they bought tickets for the 10:00 show.

In the grandstand, they were surrounded by many children and their parents. The children carried expensive cameras and snacked on ice cream and candy.

"**They** certainly don't need Christmas," Santa muttered to his wife.

They watched while dolphins leapt out of the water and small whales circled the tank with trainers riding on their backs.

"This is the life!" sighed Santa.

The following day, Santa decided that they should take a bus tour of the city. "Santa, do you think that I should bring a sweater?" asked Mrs. Claus.

"Don't call me Santa! I'm Mr. Claus now," he informed her, putting on slacks, a Hawaiian shirt with flamingoes on it, and sunglasses.

The tour bus was packed with sightseers. It traveled near an inland waterway where expensive homes sat beneath tropical trees. Lush flowers were planted everywhere and motor boats and launches were moored at docks out in front.

"It's easy to see that they don't need Christmas **here**," he commented.

The tour bus drove along the ocean front, where famous resort hotels were built on private, sandy beaches. There were signs in front of them advertising appearances by well-known entertainers.

"Don't even mention Christmas," Mr. Claus muttered under his breath.

The tour bus came to a sign that said "Detour." The driver turned to the passengers.

"Sorry about the delay, folks. We're going to have to drive through some streets in the less glamorous part of town. Don't worry — you'll be perfectly safe and we will soon be back on the main road."

The bus turned off the highway and went down some shabby streets. The buildings lining the road were grim. Dirty, barefoot children stood in front of the dilapidated houses.

Mr. and Mrs. Claus became quite nervous. There were more slum buildings and children of all colors played in the debris alongside the curb.

Mr. Claus couldn't stand it. "Stop the bus!" he roared.

"No!" the driver insisted. "I have orders never to stop in this section of the city."

"I SAID STOP THE BUS!" Mr. Claus shouted, his white locks flying about his face, his chest flung out in anger.

The door opened and Mr. Claus got out of the bus. He approached a little boy who was sitting on a splintery porch, playing with a broken truck.

"Young fellow," he began. The boy looked up. "I want to ask you a question. What do you hope to get for Christmas this year?"

The boy looked sad. He rubbed his head. "I won't be getting anything," he replied. "My family came here from Puerto Rico a month ago and we have no money to spend on Christmas. My father is sick and cannot work."

"No Christmas?" Mr. Claus's voice quavered. "But Florida is such a rich place. Everyone must be able to afford Christmas."

"Not my family," the boy said. "Mister, who are you? Why are you asking these things?"

"I'm just a tourist," he replied gruffly.

Mr. Claus got back on the bus and his wife could see that he was very unhappy.

The tour bus swung off the detour and entered a nicer section of town where immense cruise ships were docked. People were boarding them for trips to the Bahamas.

Mr. Claus could hardly wait to finish the tour.

"This is terrible!" he exclaimed to Mrs. Claus. "I've been a selfish fool."

"But what is the matter?" she asked.

"I've been thinking only of myself and how much I needed a vacation. I've ignored the poor children all over the world who will not have Christmas! I pretended that they did not exist. Well, I've come to my senses. Pack our clothes as soon as we get to the hotel. We're going home!"

"Oh, Santa," she said, kissing his white mustache. "I'm so glad!"

But it was very late. It was December 22nd and Christmas Eve was only two days away.

They hurriedly checked out of the hotel and took a taxi to the airport. The terminal was jammed with people traveling north for the holidays. The Clauses went from line to line in front of each ticket window.

"We have no seats available," they were told over and over again. "You must have reservations."

"But we must get to Chicago! This is an emergency!" Santa pleaded.

"They all say that," sniffed the clerk.

"What will we do?" asked Mrs. Claus.

"We'll keep on trying," declared her husband. "We are going to the Pole!"

Once again, they checked the ticket booths near the crowds of travelers waiting with suitcases and duffel bags. There was nothing.

Mrs. Claus sat down on a bench and began to cry.

"What's the matter, my dear lady?" inquired a man sitting near her.

Mrs. Claus took off her glasses and wiped them. "We must be in Chicago as soon as possible. It's extremely urgent and there are no seats on any of the planes."

"My wife and I are scheduled to visit her sister in Illinois," said the man. "But the weather reports have discouraged us. We hate all that snow and ice. We've been trying to decide whether or not to cancel the trip.......What do you say, Dear?" he asked his wife. "Shall we stay in Florida?"

"Oh please, let's go home," she said.

"You can buy our tickets," he said to Mrs. Claus.

"You wonderful man!" Mrs. Claus exclaimed, hugging him.

The Clauses were able to board a jet, but many hours passed before they were in Chicago. Santa worried all the way. "What if I've come to my senses too late?"

When they landed in Chicago, snow was falling and the winds were strong. There were Christmas decorations everywhere and holiday wreaths in the airport shops.

They were able to get seats on a plane for Fairbanks. Very few people were going to Alaska for Christmas.

But now it was really *very* late. It was the 24th of December. The land was buried beneath heavy, frozen snow.

Mrs. Claus shivered in her light coat.

"There isn't time to take the bus and ride in my old car to the Pole," declared Santa.

"What will we do? We have so little time left before midnight."

"I'm chartering a helicopter!" stated Santa.

"We can't afford that," his wife protested.

"It must be done. There's no other way!"

Santa dashed all over the airport until he finally located a helicopter pilot who was willing to fly them both to the North Pole for a considerable sum of money.

"I'm an adventurer," the pilot boasted. "I've flown in war zones and I used to fly tours over the Grand Canyon. I'll go anywhere! Even to the North Pole!"

Through the helicopter windows, nothing could be seen but the frozen landscape stretching for miles beneath them. There were no towns or houses, just snow driven by the howling winds.

Then far off, a distant light twinkled. It was their small, brown house with the workshop and the barn beside it, almost covered with snow.

They disembarked and fought their way through the fierce wind to the front door. The elves opened the door and the Clauses fell inside.

"Welcome, and Merry Christmas!" they cried. "We knew you would return in time. The reindeer are hitched up and the sleigh is loaded. We've been waiting for you!"

Santa dashed into the bedroom and quickly donned his red suit and hat.

"Don't forget your bag!" his wife shouted as he raced out the door.

The reindeer were pawing the snow, eager to begin the flight. They looked frisky and their breath sent frosty plumes into the air. The sleigh was heaped with presents. Santa leaped in.

Inside the house, the clock struck midnight as Santa urged the deer into the air. As they crossed the face of the moon, he called, "I'm coming, children! It's Christmas! Christmas forever!"